What was Indiana Jones doing in Great Britain on Halloween of 1913?

Indiana Jones is that world-famous, whip-cracking hero you know from the movies...

But was he *always* cool and fearless in the face of danger? Did he *always* get mixed up in hair-raising, heart-stopping adventures?

Yes!

Read all about Indy as a kid. Follow him as he unearths a dirty plot in a Welsh coal mine—and steps back in time to the days of King Arthur...And get ready for some edge-of-your-seat excitement!

Young Indiana Jones books

YOUNG INDIANA JONES

and the
GHOSTLY RIDERS

By William McCay

Random House 🏠 New York

Copyright © 1991 by Lucasfilm Ltd. (LFL)
All rights reserved under International and Pan-American Copyright
Conventions. Published in the United States by Random House, Inc.,
New York, and simultaneously in Canada by Random House of Canada
Limited, Toronto.

Young Indy novels are conceived and produced by Random House, Inc., in
conjunction with Lucasfilm Ltd.

Library of Congress Cataloging-in-Publication Data
McCay, William. Young Indiana Jones and the ghostly riders / William
McCay.   p. cm.
Summary: In 1913 young Indiana Jones finds an ancient silver ring that may
have belonged to King Arthur, investigates sabotage of a Welsh friend's coal
mines, and travels back in time to solve a crisis in the present.
ISBN 0-679-81180-X (pbk.)   ISBN 0-679-91180-4 (lib. bdg.)
[1. Adventure and adventurers—Fiction. 2. Time travel—Fiction.]
I. Title   PZ7.M1292Yr   1991 [Fic]—dc20 90-53241

Manufactured in the United States of America   10 9 8 7 6 5 4

TM & © 1991 Lucasfilm Ltd. (LFL). All rights reserved.

YOUNG INDIANA JONES™

and the

GHOSTLY RIDERS

Chapter 1

"Next time we go to the top of the bell tower, we take the stairs," grunted young Indiana Jones. With one hand, he clung to a spike driven into the stone wall of the tower. His feet rested on spikes too. They were driven in in a diagonal line, like crude steps.

Indy's other hand had a firm hold on the belt of his pal, Cerdic Sandyford. That was just as well—because Cerdic's wildly waving hands were trying to clutch thin air.

Indy fought the deadly pull of Cerdic's weight until his friend caught his balance again. "Blasted spike came right out of the wall!" Cerdic gasped. "That never happened in the book I read where the fellas climbed like this."

He glanced back at Indy, a little embarrassed. "Look, old bean. Maybe I should go on alone. It will only take me a second to nip up to the top of the tower and get my books." Cerdic pointed at the hole in the stone where the spike had been. "And maybe it's a bit wiser to keep the traffic on my spike stairway as light as possible."

"You're sure you'll be all right?"

Cerdic grinned. "Right as rain. I've made the climb dozens of times. This is the first time I've almost fallen and broken my neck."

Staring down for a second, Indy shook his head. I'm only fourteen—and too young to die, he thought. The tower was the highest point in Charenton Academy, but it didn't look too tall from the ground. Hanging to a spike on the outside of the tower gave Indy a whole new view of the forty-foot drop. And the chill late-October breeze made him even more uncomfortable.

Why Cerdic hid his library books up in the tower, Indy didn't have a clue. But they had to get them down before they could leave for the term break. Otherwise, they wouldn't be heading off to visit Cerdic's family in Wales. And they'd better hurry. The train was leaving soon.

Indy started down the spikes while Cerdic scrambled up. By the time Indy reached the ground, his friend had already disappeared into the open windows of the belfry.

Indy stared up, then glanced at the paths leading around the chapel. They were empty. He suddenly realized that this was the kind of prank that got kids kicked out of strict schools like Charenton Academy.

To tell the truth, Indy wouldn't have minded leaving the school. Almost all the British boys had been downright nasty to him and his friend, Herman Mueller. The only boy who'd made friends with "the Yanks" had been Cerdic Sandyford.

Cerdic had stepped up to Indy on the first day of classes. "You're Henry Jones," he said eagerly. "Are you related to *the* Henry Jones?

The author of *The Quest of Gawain* and *Search for the Holy Grail*?"

"That's my dad." Henry was Indy's real name, and he hated it. "Call me Indy—it's short for Indiana Jones."

Cerdic pumped Indy's hand vigorously. "A pleasure, Indy. I've read every one of your father's books. Medieval history, the age of King Arthur—they fascinate me. Oh, by the way, I'm Cerdic Sandyford."

"Cedric?" Indy frowned uncertainly.

Cerdic gave him a good-natured grin. "Everyone says that, you know. Not Cedric. It's *Cerdic*—a very old British name. Dates back fifteen hundred years, to the days before King Arthur—before there even was an England."

That was the beginning of an odd friendship. Cerdic kept surprising Indy—like today. Just when Indy thought his pal was a bookish sort, Cerdic would come up with something like this spike stairway. "I read about it in *Men of Iron*," Cerdic explained. Indy knew the book—it was a story about young men training to become knights. The trainees—squires—had set up a secret clubhouse in a castle tower. The only way in or out was by climbing spikes hammered into the tower walls.

Cerdic's head now appeared in the window, and he scanned the area to make sure the coast was clear. He climbed down from the top of the tower, a leather book bag hanging from his neck. In a moment, he stood beside Indy, grinning.

"Did you *have* to leave your books up there?" Indy asked, staring up at the tall stone structure.

"I like to read in private," Cerdic explained.

"Couldn't we have gotten up some other way?"

"There's a stairway—on the inside, of course," Cerdic admitted. "But there's a bit of a problem. It's behind a locked door, and only the headmaster has the key."

Indy had been at Charenton for only two months. But he already knew that the headmaster, Dr. Chadwick, was a quick hand with the whipping cane.

"Lucky he didn't catch us, eh?" Cerdic said, heading for the library. "Come on, Indy."

Sighing, Indy followed. Cerdic had invited him to visit his family's mine out in Wales for the term break—a short holiday around Halloween. Herman was visiting with his father in London during a halt in Mr. Mueller's archeological dig. Professor Jones was still stuck with his classes at Oxford. Actually, Indy didn't mind. He hoped to do some archeological digging himself—Cerdic had promised to show him lots of interesting sites.

Right now, they had to dash for the library, drop off the books, then grab their bags at the dorms. Cerdic had a horse-drawn cab waiting at the gate, but they still had to rush to the train station.

The train to Wales was just about to leave. Puffs of steam jetted from the locomotive. Whenever Indy got on a British train, he was reminded that he wasn't in America anymore. Rather than having rows of seats, English rail cars were divided into compartments. Indy and Cerdic walked down a long corridor, peeking into the small four-seat cubicles.

Finding an empty compartment, they sat facing each other. Indy finally asked a question that had been bothering him. "How did you manage to nail those spikes into the stone in the first place?"

Cerdic gave him a shy smile. "With great difficulty," he admitted. "It was hard hammering them in one-handed while muffling the noise. I can handle a hammer, though. My father insisted that I learn to handle a hammer and chisel, just like the miners at our colliery—coal mine, I guess you'd call it. It's a lot easier to hammer with both feet on the ground."

Indy blinked. "Your dad wanted you to learn how to hammer like a coal miner?"

"Father wanted me to know how hard our people work to get the coal out of the ground. We make money from the mine, but we owe much to the people—our miners."

The train was now huffing and puffing across the county of Somerset. Outside the window were wide vistas of flat, open plain. Every once in a while, a hill would rise out of the stubble fields of harvested grain, like an island in a golden sea.

"This is real King Arthur country," Cerdic said, gazing out. "It was a stronghold for the Celts—the ancient people who lived in Britain. Fifteen hundred years ago, when the Angles and Saxons invaded, this is where some of my Celtic ancestors made a stand. Most of the hills had strongholds on top. In fact, we're passing one of the most famous hill-forts right now—Cadbury Castle."

The train tracks curved, taking the train around a sizable rise—a good five stories tall. One look told Indy that humans had been at work on this hill. Although the lower slopes were thickly forested, he could see that the hillside rose in four terraces, like giant steps.

"Somebody did a lot of digging there," Indy said. "But I don't see any castle."

"If you're expecting a stone fortress, too bad," Cerdic said. "The whole hill was a fort, with the defenses dug in. There were four earthen ramparts surrounding the plateau on top."

His eyes shone. "I've read that this year, they've just begun the first real archeological dig here. Who knows what it will find? The local people have legends that this is the site of Camelot—King Arthur's capital."

Indy studied the high ridge carefully as it disappeared behind them. "I guess my dad's heard all about those legends."

"I learned them all on my grandfather's knee," Cerdic said. "My family originally came from Somerset. It was my great-grandfather who took some money from our family estate and invested it in Welsh coal. We still have the old estate. Many's the time I'd sit with Grandfather and hear stories."

He grinned. "My favorite was about Arthur's ghostly riders. Every seven years, so the tale goes, a cavalcade of misty figures sets off from the old entrance to the hill-fort. It's happened for centuries, and it always happens on the same date."

"Let me guess," Indy said, laughing. "Midsummer Eve? Arbor Day?"

"Oh no, old bean." Cerdic shook his head. "Halloween. It's the eve of the ancient Celts' New Year's feast—Samhaim."

He told more stories and legends of King Arthur as they chugged along into more hilly country. "No one really knows who King Arthur was," Cerdic said. "Some people even think he was a Roman named Artorius."

When they arrived at Bristol, the boys changed trains. Then they crossed a river on a huge steel railroad bridge. Passing another city, they entered into more mountainous country. "Welcome to Wales," Cerdic said. "A different countryside, a different people . . ."

"Even a different language," Indy added, staring out as the train pulled into a small station. "How do you pronounce the name of this place?" A sign on the platform read LLANTRISANT.

"The language is Cymric." Cerdic pronounced the word like Kim-rik. "The people call this land Cymru. 'Wales' and 'Welshman' are actually ancient English words—for calling these people 'strangers.' "

The mountains grew more rugged—dark, gray stone peaks that seemed almost black. "We're heading into the Vales of Rhondda,"

Cerdic said. "Soon we'll be stopping at Trewen, where the colliery is."

Indy had noticed little green valleys between the peaks. But now the valleys became ash gray. Even the sky seemed gray, as if the plume of smoke from the locomotive had somehow filled the upper air.

Then he realized it was smoke. Some of it came from the chimneys of little mining towns. But mainly the smoke was from huge ovens at the coal mines themselves. He'd read about "cooking coke"—making high-grade special coal product. He'd just never realized how smoky it was.

The crooked streets, the grim gray rock of the houses, the constant gritty feel in the air. All of it made the whole region seem faded and ashy. "So these are the coal fields," Indy finally said. "I feel like I've died and gone to the wrong place."

Cerdic nodded. His face was serious as he gazed out the window. "Things are a little better at Trewen—at least at my father's mine." He frowned. "But there are people who'll ruin anything to make a few more pennies. And they punish whoever won't go along with them. Father's last letter mentioned that someone had wrecked a water pump at the mine. He's got a tunnel flooded now, because he tries to make things better, not worse."

The train tracks curved down a mountainside to the mouth of a small valley. Indy could see a platform with a little stone station house. Window boxes full of flowers seemed to defy the grayness around them.

"Here's the station. Let's get our bags." The train jerked to a stop, and Cerdic threw open the outside door of their compartment. "There's no denying that coal-getting is a dirty, dangerous business," he said as they stepped onto the platform. "Some of the places here even use children to do the work. But not in our mine. It's a grown man's job—that's what we hire, and we give them good wages. We even built a bathhouse so they can clean up before heading home. And when he's down there, my father—"

"Your father is a fool," a voice boomed from beside them.

Indy and Cerdic whirled, to find a large, stout man glaring at them. The man had big, flabby jowls, which a black mustache and side whiskers didn't hide. His face was red, and his thick lips were curled in a sneer.

The man went on in a lower tone, almost growling now. "In fact, your father is the worst kind of fool—the can't-leave-well-enough-alone sort. Take it from me, boy, his soft heart will cost him his mine, his fortune—*everything*!"

Chapter 2

Indy stared in astonishment at Cerdic's tight face as the fat man stomped heavily across the station platform. An old-fashioned black carriage was pulled up by the steep road, obviously awaiting him. The coachman hastened to open the door and help the big man into it.

"Who *is* that guy?" Indy whispered to Cerdic.

"Mr. Gorham—Charles Gorham. He's the manager at the Sydney Colliery. It's owned by a big London company."

"Seems like a real friendly man," Indy said. "Does he always talk to you like that?"

Cerdic shrugged. "Since he arrived two years ago, Mr. Gorham hasn't seen eye to eye with my father on how to deal with the miners. He seems to see them more as—" Cerdic frowned. "Slaves, I suppose you would say. He doesn't mind how many of them get sick, or hurt—as long as the coal keeps coming out."

"I can see where that might not go with the way your father does things," Indy said. "But why is this Gorham guy so upset about it?"

"He's organized something called the Managers' League—it's an organization of all the mine managers in the area. Well, almost all. Father says that Gorham is using it to coordinate moves against the miners. You know—'present a united front, and we can grind them down even further.' That sort of thing."

"So your father won't go along?" Indy said.

Cerdic nodded. "Gorham says he's soft on the workers—holding back the other mines.

Father's the only owner hereabouts who actually lives near his mine and manages it for himself. He sees how the people live—and doesn't have to please some owner off in a distant city. I'm glad Father is here to stand up to the managers for the workers," he said defiantly. "Otherwise, Gorham would push through lots more of his nasty ideas on how to run the mines."

"Well, judging from the way Gorham is acting, your dad must be doing a pretty good job." Indy picked up his bag. "So which way do we walk?"

"Is that young Mr. Cerdic?"

The voice came from the door of the station house. A handsome young man in a pepper-and-salt tweed suit waved to Cerdic, then stepped over. He took off his cloth hunting cap, smoothing back blond hair. Indy noticed a carefully clipped mustache over the man's cheerful grin.

"This is Eric Wace, our mine engineer," Cerdic said. "Eric, this is Indiana Jones."

"Indiana?" Wace raised his eyebrows. "Sounds American to me." He smiled and shook hands. "I had business with the stationmaster, and was afraid you'd left already. We got a new piston rod for the water pump in Number Three Tunnel. The old rod was cut—looks like a nasty bit of sabotage."

He glanced back at the station house. "In fact, you two strapping lads could help me move it onto the wagon."

The wooden box containing the long rod was heavy. But with three of them lifting, it was an easy enough job to carry it to a fair-sized, sturdily built wagon standing in the road. Half asleep in the harness were a pair of stocky ponies who looked as if they'd hardly be able to move the weight behind them.

Wace climbed into the wagon, motioning for the boys to push the box toward him. "We'll just lay it down on this bed of hay— no sense in getting the blasted thing bent now." He grunted as he took the weight of the box, then set it down. "Fine. Now throw your bags on top, climb aboard, and we'll be off."

"Are you sure we aren't overloading these little horses?" Indy asked.

Wace laughed. "These Welsh ponies may

not look like much, but they'll surprise you with how strong they are."

He shook the reins, clicking his tongue a couple of times. The ponies pricked up their ears, nickered, and leaned into the harness. Soon they were heading along the station road at a good pace.

The road led to a stone bridge over a small river, then branched off. One side headed off toward the mine. "We'll see you fellows home first, then deliver this rod." Wace followed the second road, which climbed steeply up the side of the valley. Above him, Indy could make out a whole little town clinging to the side of the slope. Streets and stone houses rose like steps to the top of the valley.

Below, on the valley floor, the coal workings spread out in all their grimy glory. Indy had seen pictures of mines. He recognized the pithead, a tower with a huge pulley at the top. Two steam elevators were in constant use, the big cable winches winding and unwinding as cars went up or down. From out of the ground cartloads of coal either went to be piled into railway gondolas or were loaded into the coke ovens. The ovens belched huge clouds of gray smoke, staining the mine buildings, the houses on the hillside, even the sky above.

Indy shook his head. Cerdic hadn't said the half of it when he described coal mining as dirty. A steam whistle blew, and men, instead of coal, began emerging from the pithead. The miners looked weary and filthy as they made their way to the surface. Coal dust stained their clothes, and mixed with sweat to paint their faces. In spite of the early fall chill in the valley, the inside of the mine must have been sweltering.

For every group of tired miners that climbed out of the elevator, a new group—fresher, cleaner-looking—came in. Indy realized the mine must be run round the clock.

Eric Wace had followed Indy's eyes as the wagon jounced its way up the road. "Changing of the guard, what?" he said, running a finger along his clipped mustache.

"From the way you wear your mustache—and the way you talk—you seem like a military man," Indy said.

"Spot-on," Wace said, looking a little surprised. "You must read all those detective stories or something." Slipping the reins to his left hand, he snapped a crisp, military salute with his right. "Ex-lieutenant Eric Wace, at your service."

Then he grinned. "I was with the sappers—nowadays, I think you Yanks call them combat engineers."

"That's not exactly close to mining for a living," Indy said.

"Oh, it's closer than you might imagine." Wace laughed. "There's no great difference between digging a trench—or a tunnel under enemy walls—and digging a tunnel down for coal. It's a deeper tunnel here, of course—that makes it a bit more dangerous. On the other hand, you don't have a lot of enemies digging a tunnel toward you to blow you up or shoot you."

"How dangerous is coal-getting?" Indy asked.

Wace's smile faded. "Dangerous enough. Coal lies in seams, far under the ground. That's why the mining takes place in valleys. The ground's lower there—closer to the coal. Anyway, you dig a pit into the earth, then cut access tunnels sideways to find the coal. The pressure of the rock on the tunnels is tremendous. Tunnels would collapse if we didn't shore them up with timbers. We leave pillars of rock—sometimes, even of unmined coal."

He shook his head. "Not a nice thought, strolling down a dark cave, thinking about tons of rock pressing down on you. And then there's the coal-getting itself. We mine what's called a longwall, which runs at right angles to the access tunnels. The place that's being worked at the moment is called the face. You'd have a long walk to the face, usually, because it's the farthest spot from the elevator pit. As you dig out the coal you retreat back toward the pit."

"Seems simple enough," Indy said.

"Ah, but where you pull coal out of the seam, you leave an empty space—that caves in." Wace pointed farther down the valley, where in several areas the ground had seemingly sunk. "Subsidence, it's called. The rock above just smashed the old minings flat. Those bad sections date back to the old days.

Since Mr. Sandyford took over, we try to fill in finished longwalls with digging waste."

Indy noticed that the subsidence wasn't as bad closer toward the pithead. "But the ground still goes down," he pointed out.

Wace shrugged. "That shows you what the pressure can do. We pack the mined-out tunnels full, but the pressure of the rocks above presses down our fill to half size."

Indy shivered. Eric Wace didn't make the Sandyford mine sound like an inviting place to visit or explore.

"We've been very lucky about cave-ins on tunnels we actually use," Wace went on. "Last one happened before I came here—only three men died." He shook his head again. "Ugly business, that."

Cerdic spoke up. "Indy, you don't have to go down if you don't want to," he said. "I mean, it's beastly dark and dirty down in the colliery. And I daresay we'll just be in people's way."

He pointed up to the top rim of the valley. "You'll be able to see that there's still some green in the hills. We can go riding, and I'll show you—"

28

Cerdic never got a chance to finish his promise. Indy heard a sharp *thwap!*—something like a loud slap. Then the right-hand pony suddenly gave a loud, panicked neigh and reared in its harness.

The reins tore out of Wace's grasp as the suddenly wild horse kicked and reared, forcing its teammate to slew around. The whole wagon teetered as one wheel went off the steep road.

Another *thwap!* and now both horses were acting crazy, jumping around, kicking back at the wagon.

"Jump!" Wace yelled, rising up in the driver's seat.

The wagon lurched, and they were thrown back. They heard the creaking of wood. Then came an ominous *crack!* as the wooden wagon shafts gave way.

The wagon—with Wace, Cerdic, and Indy still aboard—went careening back down the steep, rocky road.

Chapter 3

Eric Wace had been reaching for the trailing reins when horses and wagon parted company. Indy tried to grab for him. But Wace was already out of reach, tumbling forward into a somersault.

Luckily, the wagon was going one way and the horses the other. Wace landed hard, rolling on the rocky roadbed. The wagon rattled wildly as it picked up speed. Then Indy and Cerdic saw Wace running after them. But the man was quickly left behind.

"What are we going to do?" Cerdic asked, his face pale.

Indy clung to the wooden seat as they bounced crazily. "Break our necks, if we keep going at this speed." He moved to the driver's side of the seat. "Let's see if we can slow down a little."

A thick wooden stick rose up at the end of the driver's seat. Indy grabbed it and heaved. The other end of the stick pressed into the right front wheel, acting as a crude brake. The wagon swerved and shook from side to side, nearly flinging Indy from the brake control. They were starting to slow down, however.

Cerdic yelled, "The road curves here! We're not going to make—"

"We've got to jump—now!" Indy battled with the brake lever as Cerdic jumped. Then he leapt himself.

The harsh impact with the stony road knocked the wind out of Indy, and scraped his palms. He wobbled to his knees just in time to see the wagon reach the curve in the road—and fly off.

The wagon plunged over the lip of the road, hung there for a second, then began rolling broadside down the valley, over and over

31

again. A boulder halted the wagon's progress. It hit, rebounded, then hit again, smashing itself to bits.

Indy staggered over to the edge of the road for a better view, and Cerdic joined him. "That—that could have been us!" Cerdic stared down at the wreckage in shock.

"Boys! Thank heavens you're all right!" a panting voice gasped behind them. Eric Wace was still breathing hard from his run down the hill after them. He'd lost his hat, his hair was mussed, his tweeds torn and stained.

Combing his hair back with his fingers, the young engineer stared down at the wrecked wagon. "Total loss, I'd say." He started carefully making his way down the slope, sliding on some of the more abrupt drops.

"Why—?" Indy began.

"The piston rod!" Cerdic began the scrambling descent as well. A moment later, Indy followed.

He caught up with Eric Wace as the engineer peered over the splintered side of the wagon. Wace's face was taut, and Indy soon saw why. The long wooden box had been thrown from its bed of hay, right against the

32

boulder that had stopped the wagon. Not only was the box shattered, the piston rod was bent.

"A week's waiting lost," Wace said. "And it means the Number Three Tunnel will stay flooded until we get another replacement."

He shook his head, almost in despair. "Let's at least rescue your luggage, lads. Then we hoof it up the road so we can get the news to Mr. Sandyford."

They hadn't gotten much closer to the Sandyford house when they met Cerdic's father himself. Mr. Sandyford and a couple of servants came cantering down the road on horseback. Cerdic's father was probably a picture of what Cerdic would look like in twenty years. The elder Sandyford had the same thin, angular good looks, the same lean yet tough body, the same dark skin and eyes. Unlike his son, though, Sandyford senior had flecks of gray in his black hair. He also had the dark marks that lack of sleep leaves under a person's eyes.

"Cerdic—Wace!" he cried, reining in his horse when he saw them on the roadway. "We saw the horses come running up the hill in broken harness—so I knew there would be trouble. We have rope and tackle with us—there's no one hurt, is there?"

"No, sir." Wace's voice was that of a junior officer reporting to the colonel. "And I'm sorry to say, there's no need for the rope and tackle either. The wagon is smashed—and the piston rod warped—beyond repair."

Mr. Sandyford's shoulders sagged. Indy thought he looked even more tired than before. Then a flash of anger came across the man's face. "It's not enough that someone sabotages our water pump. Now we lose the replacement part in an accident. Number Three Tunnel will be completely under water before we'll be able to start pumping."

He sighed. "Wace, we'll now have to find a way to keep those men from Tunnel Three working. I won't hear of chucking them out."

Wace looked doubtful. "I don't know what we can do. There's just not enough work in the other two tunnels to take up all those men. They'll only be getting in the way. I'd be afraid of accidents. . . ."

"I'd be afraid of more sabotage, sir," Indy put in.

Cerdic quickly introduced Indy to his father. "What do you mean, young man?" Mr. Sandyford asked.

"I think you'll find that the ponies who pulled this wagon were hurt." Indy frowned. "They didn't go wild by themselves. Someone shot rocks at the horses, to make them act up."

"You're saying the rod was destroyed deliberately—and that you lads, and Eric, might have been killed." Mr. Sandyford shook his head. "It's bad enough that someone is trying to close down the mine. But the worst part is that it has to be an inside job. Only one of the workers could sabotage the pump. Only people I trusted knew when we were getting the replacement rod. He's not merely a cad, but a traitor."

Riding double behind a servant, Indy finally arrived at Sandyford Lodge, Cerdic's home. The sun had almost set, but in the purplish light, Indy made out a comfortable, rambling old house, with a carefully tended garden in front.

Servants held oil lamps to light the way. Mrs. Sandyford stood in the midst of the

35

group. Her face was pale under brown hair pulled back in a bun, and her dark eyes were filled with worry.

"Darling!" she called to her husband. "What happened?"

Mr. Sandyford related the story, with additions by Cerdic and Eric Wace. Indy watched the tall, handsome woman take everything in.

"Cerdic, you could have been killed!" she exclaimed as her son explained how he had leapt from the wagon. "But we've all the more reason to be thankful to Mr. Jones for slowing down the wagon." Mrs. Sandyford's voice was gentle, with an odd, lilting accent that Indy couldn't identify.

"Jones," she went on, smiling at Indy. "That's a fine old Cymric name—do you know where your people come from?"

Indy could only shrug. "My father could tell you everything you'd ever want to hear about King Arthur. But I'm afraid he's not very big on family history."

"King Arthur, is it?" Mrs. Sandyford said, glancing from Indy to Cerdic. "I can see how you so quickly became my son's friend."

"If we can borrow some ponies, I'd like to show Indy the Throne and the Fountain tomorrow," Cerdic said eagerly. Indy could hear the capital letters on Throne and Fountain.

Mrs. Sandyford laughed. "Well, I'd have to say you came through the mishap well enough. Why don't you wash up, clean some of those scrapes, and get some supper in you. Then we'll decide how you'll spend tomorrow."

The two boys glanced at one another. They'd already made up their minds without even having to speak. Part of this visit would be spent doing some archeology. But they'd also poke around to find out who was trying to wreck the Sandyford mine.

By the next morning, Indy was only a little sore from the previous evening's leap for life. And even those small aches and pains were forgotten in the excitement of getting out to explore. Cerdic led the way to the kitchen, where they had an enormous breakfast. The cook also gave them a covered picnic basket for lunch.

"This will be ripping good fun," Cerdic said, carrying the basket as they headed for the stables. A pair of ponies had been prepared, and Cerdic carefully tied the basket to his saddle.

"I told Toby, the stableboy, to put the folding shovel on your horse," he told Indy. "I don't know if we'll actually do any digging, but we'll be ready if we do."

Moments later, they were setting off into the hills. As they headed away from the valley, Indy saw a little more greenery. But in the distance, he saw other small valleys, each with a cloud of coal smoke over it.

Cerdic followed his gaze, and shook his head. "Once this was all green—farming country. The coal-getting has brought some money here—and a lot more people than used to live in these valleys."

Indy stared at the harsh black mountains ahead of them. "You'd think no one would live in this country."

"People have lived here for thousands of years," Cerdic told him. "Not always by choice, of course."

"What do you mean?"

"Sometimes people were driven into these hills. When the Romans invaded back in A.D. 43, it was the British tribes in the hills that gave them the hardest fight. Then, after the Romans pulled back from Britain and the Saxons invaded, many of the native Celts were driven into the mountains and valleys of Wales."

"Not all at once, though," Indy said. "Didn't King Arthur stop the invaders?"

Cerdic nodded. "For a while. Arthur was the greatest Celtic leader. He commanded the British forces in twelve battles to defeat the Angles and Saxons. The invaders were held back for nearly fifty years. But the Britons couldn't work together. In the end, they were driven out to hold on to the mountainous edges of the island—Cornwall, Wales, and Scotland. Their old country became known by the name of one of the conquering tribes— Angle-land."

"England," Indy translated. "Well, I guess I can see why King Arthur would be a big hero in Wales. He beat the bad guys the Welsh had to fight."

"Arthur appears in many Welsh legends,"

Cerdic agreed. "He's also mentioned in Welsh histories. And of course, every part of Wales has an Arthur's This or Arthur's That."

He smiled. "That's what I'll show you today."

They rode deeper into the hills, until they faced a tor—a stony, craggy outcrop, more mountain than hill. Cerdic pointed to the Hill's crest. "There."

"What?" Indy asked.

"Arthur's Throne," Cerdic explained.

"Well, he'd certainly have a good view when he sat down," Indy said.

They took their horses to the top of the rocky tor. There was no building—exactly. Instead, Indy found a trio of rough stones acting as uneven pillars, with a flatter boulder making a roof of sorts. Beneath was a smaller, square rock—like a seat under a stone tent.

But Indy couldn't believe that someone had arranged all those tons of rock to throw a little shade.

"Do you really think King Arthur used to sit around on that rock?" he asked in disbelief. "It looks like it's been there from the year one."

Cerdic smiled and shrugged. "I think this is some sort of ancient shrine, to tell you the truth," he admitted. "But it makes a splendid place to stop for lunch."

Indy had to agree that this was a good idea. He and Cerdic feasted on cold chicken and apples. They washed down the food with fresh cider.

Indy plunked himself down on the stone throne. "I don't know whether Arthur sat here or not," he said. "But this is really something to see."

There didn't seem to be a house or a fence in sight. Or anything built by human hands. It could have been yesterday, it could have been a thousand years ago. The hills were beautiful in their stark way.

"Let's get back on our horses," Cerdic said. "There's something else I want you to see— about two hills farther on."

They wound their way over tracks better suited for goats than ponies, down to the base of a hill. A tall, craggy rock loomed threateningly over the trail. Somehow, a little dirt had collected on the top of the rock, where an oak tree had taken root. The tree was barely alive, waging a bizarre struggle against the rock. Ancient tree roots split the rock, while the tree's trunk, gnarled by the wind, leaned at a crazy angle off the top of the crag.

The stone face of the huge rock was a sheer drop, like a small cliff. About halfway up, Indy could make out a carving—a face? Time and dripping water had worn away most of the features.

A small trickle of water dribbled down the face of the rock, collecting in a low stone trough. There was more carving in the rock— letters, Indy realized. He couldn't make out words, though.

"It's Old Welsh," Cerdic said. "Someone carved an English translation down here about two hundred years ago." He moved his horse out of the way, and Indy could read the letter carving.

DRINK, FRIEND, AND DRINK THY FILL—THE WATER FALLS BY THE HIGH KING'S WILL. He glanced over at Cerdic. "High King?"

"It's a special term from the Celtic people who lived in Britain and Ireland—it meant the leader who ruled above the local chiefs."

"And that's what Arthur was?" Indy asked.

"He was called king and war leader," Cerdic said. "Somehow, his name got connected with this spring. It's called Arthur's Fountain, and the story has been around—well, just forever. Certainly, the carvings—the original ones—are very ancient. Some people think the face is actually a Roman carving. If you look—wait a tick, here. You're not looking at the carving at all."

Instead, Indy leaned forward in his saddle, peering into one of the cracks caused by the oak roots. "I caught a glint of something," he said, pointing. "It's deep inside the rock."

Pulling out the folding shovel, he began wedging it into the crack. His pony shied a little, and Indy almost fell off.

"Let me give it a try," Cerdic suggested. He took the shovel, and his pony stood obediently still as he dug into the crack. It widened a little as a sliver of rock came out. Something was definitely gleaming in there.

He wormed his arm into the crack, digging with his fingers.

"I've got it—whatever it is." Cerdic blew dust off the small piece of metal in his hand. "Looks to be a ring—silver and jewels!"

Indy urged his pony closer for a better look. "It's a lizard of some kind—a dragon?"

"That's the old symbol of Wales." Cerdic's voice was very eager. "We've got a real find here, Indy."

"And a one-in-a-million chance of finding it," Indy began. A loud creaking noise cut him off.

Indy and Cerdic looked up to see the ancient, wind-blasted tree teetering over them. The ponies reared, and the tree trunk came crashing down!

Chapter 4

Indy's pony bucked frantically, almost flinging him off. He ducked as a branch nearly caught him in the head. The tree crashed to the ground, branches cracking off as it landed between Indy and Cerdic.

Cerdic's pony sidestepped, and Cerdic swung wildly in his saddle, the dragon ring still glinting in his hand. "That was a near thing," he shouted to Indy. "Blasted tree would have turned us to paste!"

Indy had already calmed his pony and swung down. "I wonder if somebody gave that tree a push."

He circled to the rear of the rocky crag, trying to see if anyone was up there. Cerdic dismounted and was with him a moment later, climbing up to where the oak tree had stood—or leaned.

"No footprints." Indy shrugged. "But then, most of the dirt that was up here came down with the tree's roots."

"Maybe my digging into the crevice down there did something to the roots—unbalanced the tree, or something," Cerdic suggested.

"We can't say anything for certain." Indy shrugged again. "Maybe this was Arthur's curse for anybody who stole the ring."

Cerdic stared wide-eyed at the dragon ring, which he now wore on his right hand. "You don't really think—" he began in an awed voice.

Then he gave Indy a look. "You're having me on, aren't you?"

Indy grinned. "I think that sometimes you take this magic of the Middle Ages a bit too seriously," he said.

Cerdic grinned too, embarrassed.

"Although it *is* a little strange," Indy went

on, "for the tree to fall at that particular moment." He shook his head. "Let's forget it, though. We have other mysteries to worry about."

"You mean the saboteur?" Cerdic asked.

Indy nodded as they started riding off. "We've got to find some way to identify this guy before he strikes again."

Arriving at the top of Trewen Valley, they heard the coal mine's steam whistle giving long, mournful blasts. Cerdic's face went tight. "Something is wrong—very wrong. This isn't a shift change. Either there's been an accident—" His voice dropped. "Or a cave-in."

One glance at the valley floor told them that there were definite problems down below. The Sandyford Colliery looked like an anthill after someone had kicked it. Indy realized that the tiny figures running around the buildings were people. Both pithead elevators were going full tilt, bringing miners up to the surface.

"Nobody seems to be going down," Indy said. "They all seem to be coming up."

They galloped the rest of the way to the

Sandyford house, where Mrs. Sandyford had gathered the servants. They were all carrying bandages and extra medical supplies.

"Is it a cave-in? We just heard the warning whistle," Cerdic cried, reining in his pony.

"Your father went down to take charge when he heard the whistle," Mrs. Sandyford replied. "We haven't yet been told what the problem is."

"It doesn't look like rescue parties are going into the shaft," Indy said. "All they seem to be doing is emptying the place."

Hoofbeats came thundering up the road from town. A young miner in torn trousers and covered with coal dust jumped from the saddle, yanking off his hat.

"Dai," Mrs. Sandyford said, "did my husband send you up to tell us what's happening?"

"Yes, missus," young Dai said. "Ye needn't bring the blankets and bandages. Nobbut's been hurt."

"Why is everyone coming up out of the mine?" Indy asked.

"Air's bad," the miner said.

The boys followed Dai down to the mine,

where they found Mr. Sandyford standing beside one of the elevators. A serious-looking older man, with "foreman" written all over his features, carried a long list. "We've brought everyone out, sir. The only one down in the pit now is Mr. Wace."

Cerdic's father nodded grimly, thunderclouds gathering over his face. "That scoundrel of a saboteur—whoever he is—has wrecked the ventilation fans at the bottom of the main pit. We've had to bring everyone out of the tunnels," he explained to the boys. "Otherwise, they'd be poisoned by bad air."

A bell rang from below, and the steam winch on the elevator began running. It took long minutes for the elevator platform to arrive, but they could see the gleam of Eric Wace's helmet light while it was still far underground. The mining engineer was shaking his head, looking completely defeated.

"The fan blades have been smashed— something heavy fell on them. There's no chance of repair."

"I don't suppose we'd have a spare set of fans about," Mr. Sandyford said.

"No, sir," Eric Wace said. "Mr. Gorham

has one over at the Sydney Colliery, but I shouldn't expect—"

"No," Sandyford said. "I don't think he'd be interested in helping us." He jammed his hands in his pockets. "No getting around it. The mine will be closed until we get new fans."

"Sir," said one of the older men, "I worked in the mines before they had the great fans. All it needed was a large fire in the bottom of one of the pits, to force the air up . . ."

Wace was already shaking his head. "That only works in mines where there are no dangerous gases. But this coal seam has a lot of methane. That's why we use the electric lights, instead of candles. An open flame would blow up—"

"We have enough problems as it is, Eric," Mr. Sandyford pointed out. "Until we reopen, every worker will still get half wages." He sighed, and Indy heard him mutter, "I only hope we reopen quickly."

Dinner with the Sandyfords was not a cheerful meal. The family depended on the mine for their income—as did every family in Trewen Valley. Closing the colliery down would not be easy. "Maybe I shouldn't be here in the way," Indy suggested. "If there's a train tomorrow . . ."

"Nonsense, Indy," Mrs. Sandyford insisted. "We won't hear of hustling you off. You'll leave when it's time to return to school. Don't worry—we can afford a guest."

Still, Indy was glad to escape from the dining room. "Well," he asked Cerdic when they were safely outside, "what next?"

"A good tramp might be just the thing," Cerdic suggested.

Indy looked confused. "I thought you said everyone here works at the mine. What's this about tramps . . . ?"

"No, no, a tramp—a walk—might take our minds off things."

Indy grinned. "Sure. Maybe if we're lucky, we'll find King Arthur's key chain."

They set off in the twilight, taking another path out of the valley. The path quickly wound its way up into the hills.

"Where will this take us?" Indy asked as

they toiled up yet another hillside. It seemed as if every road in the area had its ups and downs.

"To the valley where the Sydney Colliery is run, if we keep on going," Cerdic said.

"I don't think we have to do that," Indy said. "One warm welcome from that Gorham guy is enough for me."

They did go as far as the lip of the farther valley, however. Indy wanted to see if the mines looked different. They did. Mr. Gorham's mine was much larger—and the houses where his workers lived seemed much smaller, dirtier, and run-down.

Shaking his head, Indy went to turn away. Then he froze. "What's that down there, a parade?" he asked.

A series of lights was moving along the road that snaked through the floor of the valley. Cerdic peered down into the darkness. "Those are carriage lamps," he exclaimed in surprise. "It's an entire line of coaches, moving through the valley."

"Where do you think they're headed?" Indy wondered.

"Only one place on that road—Gorham's

house. It's on the other side of the valley—"

"Let's see how quickly we can get there," Indy interrupted. "Gorham's already made threats about your mine. I don't like the looks of this. Let's find out what he's up to."

It took them a while to reach Gorham's house—more like a mansion than the Sandyford home. Indy suggested that they keep out of sight on the way there, so they lost time. As they came up to the drive Cerdic stared. "I recognize these coaches. They must belong to every mine manager in the nearby valleys."

"Every one except for your dad," Indy added quietly. "This is beginning to stink, Cerdic."

He took the lead now, showing Cerdic how to sneak right up to the wall of the house. Their target was obvious. There was an open window, and even from under the carriage where they were hiding, they could hear the murmur of many voices.

Indy's course led them from the carriage to a tree, and finally to a large rosebush by the window.

"Keep an eye out for anyone," he whispered to Cerdic, rising up to peek through the window. The curtains had been left a little disarranged by the breeze. He saw a very smoky room—most of the mine managers were puffing away on cigars, sitting around a large table.

Charles Gorham rose to his feet, rapping sharply on the table. "Gentlemen," he said, "I'm very glad you were able to attend this meeting of the League on such short notice. I have very exciting news."

Gorham's face had a very ugly smile. "As you know, the Sandyford Colliery has long been a problem. Sandyford won't join with us, and his coddling of the workers has stirred up problems at our mine."

There was a general mutter of support.

"Well, I've been taking some action." Gorham gave the group another evil smile. "At my own expense, I hired an agent to—ah—slow down operations at Sandyford's colliery."

That brought some gasps from his listeners, but Gorham raised his hands for silence. "I tried to convince Sandyford, to persuade him. Words didn't work. So I moved on to actions. I suppose you heard that the ventilation fans at Sandyford have broken down. My *agent* broke them. Since I already have your agreement not to offer any help to Sandyford, my agent is ready to complete phase two of our plan tonight."

Gorham took a long puff on his cigar while the other managers engaged in a babble of questions. Then he continued. "My man is softhearted—he wanted the colliery empty before he planted the dynamite."

Indy stared, not believing what his ears had heard.

But Gorham's contemptuous voice left no doubt about it. "He's worried about killing—but luckily, not about blasting the Sandyford Colliery to bits."

Chapter 5

Indy felt a grip like iron clamp onto his arm. "He's going to destroy the mine!" Cerdic's horrified voice breathed into his ear. "What are we going to do?"

"Well, we won't hang around here, that's for sure."

Silently and carefully, they crept away from the window. Both boys quivered with impatience to be up and running. But Indy knew it wouldn't help them to start running too soon. If they got caught now, no warning would get to the mine.

At last, they were away from Mr. Gorham's

house, and deep into the friendly night. "All right," Indy said, "let's go!"

They ran for the path that had brought them to overlook the Sydney mine. Indy found himself hating the stupid road. Why couldn't it stretch as straight and fast as possible, instead of winding all over the countryside, up and down hills?

They began taking shortcuts, sliding down steep slopes to catch up with the path later on. Once, they pushed their way through some thorny bushes. It hurt, but it cut precious seconds off the trip back to Sandyford Lodge.

When they finally arrived, the boys looked like scarecrows. Both had some new scrapes and torn clothing. Still worse, thorny twigs stuck out all over them.

"Well, don't you two look odd," Mr. Sandyford said. He was in his dressing gown, just getting ready to go to sleep. But his face was grim and wide-awake as he heard the boys' story.

"Indy, you get Mr. Wace—he's in the house next door. Cerdic, you go down to the village and get Dai. Have them meet me at

Pithead One." Mr. Sandyford turned to get dressed.

Down at the mine, Wace and Dai had the elevator machinery up and running by the time Mr. Sandyford arrived. The mine owner was accompanied by four older men. Indy recognized the foreman who'd reported that all miners had been evacuated. "I'm happy to say we have some volunteers to help search for this bomb," Mr. Sandyford said. "Eric, I hope you're coming as well."

"Oh. Of course," Wace said.

"Dai, I want you up here to run the elevator," Mr. Sandyford said. "If you hear the bell ring, we may need to get out of here quickly."

"Yessir." Dai's cloth cap was crumpled in his hands. "I'll be ready."

The search crew piled onto the elevator platform. But when Indy and Cerdic went to join them, Mr. Sandyford shook his head. "Boys, I appreciate the warning you gave us. But I can't risk your lives."

"We want to help!" Cerdic said.

"You'd help me feel much better if you

were up here," Mr. Sandyford said. "It's just too dangerous."

With the boys' bitter eyes following him, Cerdic's father climbed aboard the elevator, adjusting the lamp on his mining helmet. Soon the group of searchers had disappeared into the darkness of the pit. All Indy and Cerdic could make out were the beams from their lamps.

"It's not fair," Cerdic stormed.

"Right," said Indy. "Where do they keep those helmets?"

Cerdic gave his friend a look. "What are you up to?" he asked.

"Let's concentrate on getting our equipment. Then we work on persuading Dai."

For about the nineteenth time, Dai shook his head. "No," he repeated. "Mr. Sandyford said he didn't want ye down in the pit."

"He needs every pair of hands—and eyes—he can get down there," Indy said. "We're willing. Why can't we go?"

Dai looked at Cerdic. "Your da said ye weren't to go."

"If *your* father were down there, in danger, wouldn't you want to help him?" Cerdic looked at the young man pleadingly. "Dai, we've *got* to get down there and help."

The young Welshman gave a deep sigh, and started the elevator up. "All right, on with ye—and quickly!"

Now I know how a bucket feels when it's lowered into a well, Indy thought as the elevator descended with him and Cerdic. There was no elevator cage, only a waist-high rail enclosing the platform. Rough stone walls passed inches before their eyes, until at last, with a jolt, they arrived at a low, yawning tunnel. The beam from Indy's helmet lamp petered out only a few feet into the darkness. Both boys stood silent for a moment, facing the wall of inky blackness.

That moment of hesitation in the face of the unknown actually saved their lives. In the utter quiet, Indy heard a faint hissing sound.

"What—?" Cerdic began, but Indy shushed him.

"Listen carefully. Where's that noise coming from?"

They stepped into the tunnel, but the noise seemed to get fainter. It was like a nightmare, blundering around in darkness. The maddeningly faint sound seemed to be coming from everywhere.

"It's faded out." Cerdic voice was tight as he circled around the tunnel.

Indy headed back to the elevator. "That's because it's not in the tunnel. The noise is coming from here."

He knelt on the elevator platform, pressing his ear to it. "In fact, it's coming from *under* here."

"Well, the pit goes a little deeper,'" Cerdic began.

Indy was already on his feet, pushing the button that rang the bell high above them. The elevator jerked into motion, and the boys stared into the dark depth its movement revealed.

The bottom of the pit was about six feet below them. And now they could see what was causing the hissing noise. It was a bundle of waxy sticks—dynamite—with a foot-long, burning fuse!

Even as the boys stared in horror, the

hissing, spitting fuse got measurably shorter.

Indy jumped into the pit, scrambling down the side of the wall. It was almost like a race—who would get to the dynamite first, Indy or that little, burning spark.

If the spark won, the Sandyford mine, all the men down here—and Indy and Cerdic—would be history.

With a shock, Indy dropped to his knees on the stone floor. He grabbed the dynamite in his left hand, the fuse in his right, and yanked with all his might. The fuse tore loose. Rising to his feet, Indy stomped out the little spark still racing along the primed cord.

White-faced, Cerdic stared at the dynamite in Indy's hand.

Indy, however, poked around in the shaft, looking at scorch marks on the stone. "Whoever set this up left a fuse at least three feet long," he said. "They must do set-up explosives for a living."

"That—that was jolly well done," Cerdic finally managed to say, reaching into the pit to help Indy out. "You've saved the mine, Indy. We must tell Father."

They set off down the tunnel. Indy was still carrying the now-harmless dynamite sticks. But they hadn't gone fifty yards before they met Eric Wace.

"What are you boys doing here?" he burst out angrily, making shooing gestures. "Get back to the elevator at once. In fact, I'm going to take you up."

"That may take a couple of minutes, Mr. Wace," Cerdic said. "We had to send it back up."

Wace's face went pasty. "You mean you've left us cut off down here—?"

"We *had* to send the elevator up." Indy held out the dynamite sticks. "We had to get *this* out from under it!"

Wace flinched back. Then he leaned forward, carefully examining the bomb. "You defused it?"

"Indy tore off the fuse and stamped it out," Cerdic said proudly. "We want to show Father—"

Wace still blocked their path. "You've done a fine thing, boys," he said. "But what—what if this isn't the only bomb that was planted?"

Wace looked from the bomb to his watch, a greasy film of sweat on his face. "I still think I should take you back—"

Far in the distance, they heard a muffled *boom!* Next came the shock wave that threw them to their knees. Then came a low rumbling that seemed to fill all the tunnels.

"See? There *was* another bomb," Indy said quietly.

Both Eric Wace and Cerdic Sandyford stared nervously down the tunnel. "And the worst has happened." Wace's voice was hoarse. "It's caused a cave-in!"

Chapter 6

The tunnel was filled with grit. Dirt and coal dust hung like a fog in the air. Indy quickly pulled out his handkerchief, tying it over his mouth and nose so he could breathe. Beside him, Cerdic did the same.

Eric Wace still blocked the way before them, but Cerdic pushed past. "Are you mad?" Wace cried after them. "We've got to get out of here—the roof could come down at any second!"

"Are *you* mad?" Cerdic responded. "I'm not leaving my father and those men down here."

They plunged on into the tunnel, their lamps almost useless in the murky darkness. Indy found himself continually staggering. Sometimes the tunnel floor ran level. Other times it abruptly sloped up or down. "We follow the coal seam," Cerdic explained when Indy banged into him once. "Where it slopes, the tunnel slopes."

Ahead of them, the tunnel suddenly widened. The entrances to three passageways appeared before them.

"Tunnels One, Two, and Three," Eric Wace said as the boys hesitated.

"Well, Three is full of water," Indy said. "That was why you needed your pump."

"And I'll bet Number Two is the one that collapsed," Wace said.

He was about to lead them down the dark opening when they heard the sound of voices down Tunnel One.

"Halloooo!" Cerdic called into the darkness. "Is everyone all right?"

"It's Master Cerdic!" A voice came from the distance. "Come quick, sir!"

Indy didn't like the sound of that. Neither did Cerdic. He ran ahead, and Indy followed. The passage seemed to bump along forever. Then they saw a slightly brighter area ahead. The four miners were gathered in a knot in the middle of the shaft, looking fearfully at the ceiling of the tunnel.

"Where is my father?" Cerdic's voice seemed shockingly loud over the men's nervous muttering.

"Yonder." The foreman pointed to a boiling cloud of dust that still hadn't settled. "He was searching the mine face, and sent us back to check along the hauling roads. We found nowt, but Mr. Sandyford—he was in there when the bomb went off."

"Father!" Cerdic's cry was drowned out by a horrible creaking sound. It was the sound of tons of rock pressing in on the weakened mine ceiling.

"Softly, sir—softly!" one of the men said, looking upward. "Too much noise could bring it all down."

"The cave-in was worst in Tunnel Two," another man said. He'd lost his helmet and lamp, and had a nasty gash across his forehead. "Owen and I were lucky to get out alive."

"But it seems that Tunnel One still runs right up to the mine face," the foreman said. "There's some caving at the tunnel mouth, but it's still open."

"For how long, though?" Wace muttered unhappily. His eyes were fixed on the network of cracks working through the once-solid stone above their heads.

"You men can go back if you want," Cerdic said. "But I'm saving my father." He snatched up a pickax leaning against the wall, and continued down the tunnel.

Indy grabbed a shovel and followed. It was the longest walk of his life. Every step was punctuated by the groaning and complaining of the rocks overhead. Indy could understand why the men had been talking in whispers. Even the faintest vibration could set off a final collapse.

The going got even more treacherous as they reached the end of their journey. Boulder-sized chunks of debris blocked their path—obstructions to be bypassed or climbed over.

At last, they reached the portal to the mine face—only to find their way barred. An enormous stone slab had fallen at an angle across the entrance.

They stared at the raw hunk of rock for a moment. Indy was reminded of the massive "roof" over Arthur's Throne. This stone was even larger.

"That thing weighs tons." Cerdic slapped a hand on the rock. "There's no way we can move it."

"But maybe we can squeeze around it," Indy suggested. "This corner looks like it's full of loose rubble. Maybe if we dig it out . . ."

"Not much room," Cerdic said dubiously.

"For a grown man, no," Indy agreed. "But maybe for a skinny kid—"

"Like us!" Cerdic began carefully prying at rubble with his pickax, and Indy shoveled. Every once in a while there'd be another ominous rumble above them, but the ceiling stayed up.

"This is going to take forever." Cerdic sounded discouraged.

"Not forever, lad," a quiet voice said from behind them.

Indy and Cerdic turned to see the foreman

and the other miners, all carrying digging tools. Even a very nervous Eric Wace stood at the back of the group.

"You've come to help?" Cerdic said.

The foreman nodded. "How could we face Dai up above, telling him we'd left you down below?"

"Let us at yon rubble," one of the miners—Owen?—said. "Movin' it is what we do best."

Three miners went to work on the blockages, digging it out gently but quickly. Wace directed the foreman, Indy, and Cerdic in placing some new pillar supports.

"I don't know how long this will do any good," Wace said worriedly. "If that big boulder shifts, it may bring everything down."

The miners had cleared enough space for a very skinny young man to slip under the boulder. Cerdic pushed into the hole—and got stuck around the shoulders.

"It will have to be much bigger," he said unhappily after he wiggled back out.

"You can work on that—while I go inside." Before anyone could say a word, Indy slid into the hole. He plunged in as if he were swimming, worming his way through the darkness. The floor sloped down, then up again. For a second, the waist of Indy's pants caught in some of the loose rubble under him. He tried not to think of the tons of rock in teetering balance above him. Indy took a deep breath, sucked in his stomach, and scrabbled on.

A moment later, he popped out into the working face. There was only a small pocket left of the long transverse tunnel where the coal had been mined. And as Indy flashed his head lamp around, Mr. Sandyford wasn't in sight.

Indy's heart sank. To come so far, work so hard—and find . . .

"Indy!" Cerdic's voice echoed down the passage as the miners worked to widen it. "Have you seen my father? Is he all right?"

"I don't—" Indy began, kneeling by the opening. His lamp beam darted over a pile of rubble in front of the main cave-in. Wait—one of those dust-colored shapes wasn't a rock, it was an arm!

"Yes, I've found him!" Indy called back

down the mini-tunnel. "He's partially covered."

Indy set to work, tearing stone debris out of the way with his hands. It was like playing with a hill of sand. Remove some from the bottom, and your work is immediately filled by sand spilling down from the top.

Still, Indy managed to work his way into the pile, moving from the upper arm to free the trapped man's face. I told Cerdic this was his father, Indy thought. What if he turns out to be the saboteur, trapped in his own blast?

But no, the face he uncovered was familiar, although shockingly filthy. Under a thick layer of coal dust, Mr. Sandyford was deathly pale. Indy brought his ear close to the still man's face. Was he—?

No! He was still breathing! Indy caught the faintest trace of breath being pulled in.

He set to work with new vigor, rolling stones away with both hands, paying no attention to the little landslides he was causing. If the roof fell in, well then, it would fall. But unless Mr. Sandyford was gotten out quickly—he'd be lost.

Chapter 7

The ceiling above shuddered and sent down a fresh shower of debris. Indy huddled over Mr. Sandyford, shielding him. He could hear exclamations from outside. Was this it? Had the roof finally fallen in?

Then Cerdic came scraping out of the hole. "A little more work, and it will be wide enough—oh, *no!*" His face fell as he saw his father.

Together, they clawed at the rubble, freeing Mr. Sandyford as far as the waist.

"There doesn't seem to be anything across his legs," Indy said. "Just loose rock." He didn't like the idea of moving the man. Who knows what injuries he had? But they couldn't leave Cerdic's father here either.

"Then let's have a try at shifting him," Cerdic said. "Ready, steady—go!"

Holding him carefully by shoulder and hip, they pulled Mr. Sandyford from the rubble. It wasn't easy—the slipped rock didn't want to release its hold on the unconscious body. Indy and Cerdic were both covered with coal dust—and sweat—by the time they finally got Mr. Sandyford loose.

"So much for the simple bit," Indy said, rubbing a grimy hand across his forehead. "Now we've got to get him through that tunnel."

Cerdic looked as filthy as Indy. Little trickles of perspiration traced white lines through the grit on his face. "The men will have made it a bit wider—we'd just reached that sticky upslope when I came through."

They moved Mr. Sandyford to the tunnel entrance, and Cerdic picked up some ropes he'd left there when he'd wriggled in. "I'm going to set these up as a sort of harness around Father's shoulders," he explained. "Then I'll go in first, pulling him along. Unless—maybe you should go first."

Indy shook his head. "I'll bring up the end of the parade, ready to push if needed." He grinned at his friend. "Come on, finish those knots. We don't have all evening."

Moving Mr. Sandyford through the tunnel was a ticklish business. For one horrible instant, Indy thought the unconscious man had gotten wedged in the small opening. But with a little pushing and pulling, they got him loose.

Eager hands took on the job of drawing Mr. Sandyford out at the far end of the hole. The miners hadn't been wasting their time, having constructed a crude stretcher from tool handles and a blanket. As soon as Mr. Sandyford was freed from the cave-in, four men carried him to safety. Eric Wace stood pale-faced in the background, giving frantic orders. "Come on, come on. The rumbling is getting louder. Move!"

Cerdic grabbed Indy's arms and dragged him free. Staggering to his feet, Indy joined the stumbling rush back down the tunnel to safety.

The grinding noises above them *were* getting louder—scarier, too. Indy had just reached the trotting stretcher-bearers when the whole roof behind them gave in.

There was a *crack!* like the granddaddy of all thunder. Then came a deafening roar as countless tons of rock crashed in to fill the tunnel where they'd been barely seconds before.

None of the rescuers stopped to take in the terrifying display. The tunnel roof above them was also creaking and cracking. All they wanted now was to reach the elevator and get out of there.

Eric Wace was in the lead, tearing open the cage door around the platform. The miners carrying Mr. Sandyford hustled aboard. So did the boys. The elevator pit seemed to rock as they were slowly reeled up. A cloud of coal dust puffed out. That meant more tunnels had collapsed.

Indy felt a hand on his shoulder. He turned to see Cerdic Sandyford looking very serious. "You saved my father back there, Indy.

There's no way I can thank you." He looked down, then twisted the dragon ring off his finger. "But I can give you this. I just gave it a good polish."

The strange silver animal glinted in the light of Indy's miner's lamp. "I can't—" Indy began.

"You have to." Cerdic slipped the ring on Indy's finger. "I won't hear of you refusing."

At last, they were at the pithead, clambering out before the elevator had even stopped. Indy stared in shock. It looked as if the whole town of Trewen had showed up—all the miners, and their wives and children, surrounded the elevator.

"I blew the whistle when I heard the explosion," Dai said, a little embarrassed. "We were just getting ready to send some more folk down to help when the cave-ins began."

"Who's hurt?" an elderly woman asked, peering at the stretcher. Then she gave a shocked gasp. "Why, it's Mr. Sandyford!"

The whole crowd began clamoring when they realized their popular leader had been injured. Mrs. Sandyford pushed to the front, her face pale, her lips clamped tight. Indy saw tears trickle down her cheeks when she saw how still her husband lay.

"Dr. Padarn! Make way for Dr. Padarn!" the people cried. A small, elderly man with a fringe of white hair came up now, carrying a medical bag.

"I came as soon as I got your message," the doctor said to Mrs. Sandyford. "What happened here?"

"He was caught in a cave-in," Indy explained. "A lot of rubble fell on him."

Dr. Padarn signaled the miners to let their stretcher rest on the ground. Then, kneeling over Mr. Sandyford, he began a careful examination.

"He's alive," the doctor said, rising.

The crowd gave a sigh of relief.

"But he's in a very bad way. There's sign of concussion, and I think there may be internal injuries as well. I'll do what I can—" He glanced helplessly at Mrs. Sandyford. "But he should be in hospital. Perhaps Cardiff . . ."

Cerdic's mother shook her head decisively. "No. He's staying nowhere in Wales.

Too many powerful men here wish my husband ill. I'll take him to the estate in Somerset—out of harm's way."

Efficiently, she began making the arrangements—a carriage for her husband, Cerdic, and herself. Dr. Padarn would also come along.

"I'm sorry, Indy," she apologized. "But there won't be any room for you."

"That's all right," Indy said. "I've checked the timetable. There's a mail train that comes by later this evening. I can take that to Somerset."

"Can you—" Mrs. Sandyford paused for a moment, embarrassed. "I hate having to ask this. Can you afford to pay for your ticket? There's not much ready money in the house . . ."

"I understand," Indy said. Not much money—that was only the beginning of the problem. With the mine tunnels collapsed, the Sandyfords were just about wiped out. Their business was destroyed. And now they'd have the extra expenses of nursing Mr. Sandyford . . .

Indy thought of his return ticket to Charenton, tucked away in his suitcase. "Maybe I should just get on the train and head back to school, ma'am. I mean, I want to help any way I can, but—"

Mrs. Sandyford nodded. "But maybe the best way is to stay out of the way." She took Indy's hands. "What you did tonight was very brave. My family will always be in your debt."

Indy didn't know what to say. "Maybe when things are a little better, I'll see Cerdic at school again."

Mrs. Sandyford looked him straight in the eye. They both knew that was a polite lie. The children of bankrupt families don't go to expensive schools.

A little while later, Indy stood at the front door, shaking hands with Cerdic. "Mother told me that you'd decided to head back to Charenton early." Indy's friend tried to smile. "Don't tell me our hospitality has you homesick for the place."

Indy shook his head. "With your father and all, I think I'd just be in the way."

"Oh, I know you're just bored. You were hoping we'd poke around and find something from King Arthur's day. I rather wish we had found something—a treasure would fit the bill about now. Things will be a bit hard, otherwise." Cerdic gave up trying to joke. His handclasp became a little tighter, and he finally said, "Thanks for all the help, old bean. Must dash now. We're setting off in the carriage."

Indy waved good-bye. As he went upstairs to pack he thought he'd never seen a sadder farewell in his life.

The mail train stopped at every village, hamlet, and wide spot on the roads. Its rhythmic chugging through the night-quiet countryside sent most of the passengers to sleep.

Indiana Jones closed his eyes for the fiftieth time, and wished sleep would come to him. But it wouldn't.

Every time he closed his eyes, he saw another scene from the last couple of days. The wagon horses rearing. The tree crashing down on him and Cerdic. Mr. Sandyford, so pale and helpless in the pile of rubble. And again and again, Charles Gorham's evilly smiling face kept appearing, boasting about what he'd do to the Trewen mine.

Gorham was as guilty as the bomber who had nearly killed Mr. Sandyford. But how could they prove it? None of the other mine managers was going to talk. They were all lined up behind Gorham. If only they could have caught the saboteur! Then they'd have a witness.

Indy was the last one on for the Somerset train. His stomach had started making hungry rumblings just outside of Bristol, so he'd dashed off to get a snack at the station café. Now he was comfortably full, but almost late. He'd just managed to beat the closing gates on the platform, and jumped aboard just as the conductor was closing the compartment doors.

"That's a first-class ticket," the conductor told him. "Go on up."

Indy toted his suitcase along the corridor, trying to find an empty seat in the first-class compartments. Most were full. Many had the curtains down, with the sounds of snoring filtering through the glass windows.

Then Indy caught something else filtering into the corridor—expensive cigar smoke, just like the smoke he'd sniffed outside Charles Gorham's window.

Gorham's booming voice could be heard out in the passageway, even though the compartment door was shut. "A fine job of work, my boy. Worth every penny. Just don't gamble it away and start cheating at cards. The last time you did that, you were chucked out of the army. At least now, you can afford to be a gentleman—if not an officer."

Indy quietly made his way down the corridor until he could look into the compartment from which the scent—and sound— came.

"Go ahead," Gorham jovially suggested. "Count it. Make sure it's all there."

Indy peered through the crack between the window frame and the drawn shade. There was Charles Gorham, handing over a thick sheaf of money.

And there, taking it, was Eric Wace.

Chapter 8

It was the worst possible moment for the inside shade to roll up. But that's what happened. The shade not only flew up but it made a loud noise as it rolled.

Charles Gorham and Eric Wace whirled around—to see Indiana Jones staring at them through the compartment window.

"That boy!" Gorham yelled. "I know him—he was with Sandyford's brat!"

Wace could only sit frozen in horror, realizing that all his dirty secrets were out in the open.

Gorham smashed his agent in the arm. "What are you waiting for? Get him!"

Indy didn't wait to see how long it would take Wace to make up his mind. He just dashed down the corridor.

Halfway down the train car, he heard the sound of footsteps running after him. Wace must have decided he had no choice. That was dangerous. He'd nearly killed once—and now he had nothing to lose. If he caught up with Indy . . .

"Son—Indy—stop. I just want to talk with you," Wace called after him.

Indy ran faster.

Wace's voice got ugly. "All right, Jones. Run if you want. You can't get far, though. And when I catch up to you—"

The young engineer's threats broke off as he tripped over the suitcase Indy threw behind him.

That trick gained Indy most of the next car. But he knew Wace was right. The train had only so many cars. And where could he turn for help? Would a conductor believe his story? Or would he be more likely to listen to the rich Mr. Gorham and the military Lieutenant Wace?

Those two could even make up some story that he was traveling with them. Then, as soon as they were off the train, that would be the end of Indiana Jones.

Right now, Indy had to make sure he wasn't caught. If he managed to double back behind Eric Wace, the bad guys would have twice as much area to search. The question was, how could he do it?

Indy opened the connecting door to the next train car. There was no easy way here to climb to the roof. But . . . Indy grinned. There was another way out.

He hurried down the corridor, checking all the compartments as he passed. There—at long last, an empty one. He slid open the door and jumped inside. Then he pulled down the shades. Maybe Wace would just pass him by. He thought there was a chance—until he heard Wace's distinctive voice coming through the ventilator.

"Terribly sorry," Wace said in his best officer-and-gentleman manner. "I thought this was my compartment."

He's obviously trying every closed compartment in the carriage, Indy thought. How can I beat him?

He dashed to the lights in the compartment and turned them off. Then, under cover of the darkness, Indy quietly let the shades up. Wace was still at the other end of the car. Maybe, just maybe, this would work.

Indy opened one of the outer windows barely an inch. Then he slid open the door to the outside and stepped out of the moving train.

With one hand clinging to the windowsill and one foot wedged against the doorsill, Indy ducked down in the darkness. The door swung shut. With luck, now the compartment would look empty.

All Indy had to do was keep his precarious perch, and not fall off. The train wasn't moving at top speed. But it was chugging along fast enough to make a fall dangerous—maybe fatal.

Don't want to do Wace's work for him, Indy thought.

Even so, his fingers were getting pretty tired by the time he heard the compartment's inner door open. Indy took a deep breath. How long was Wace going to take? Then the door shut. Indy forced himself to wait another couple of seconds before he popped his head up to peek back inside. The compartment was empty.

Great! Indy thought, reaching forward with his free hand for the outer door's handle. He caught hold, pulled—and the door didn't open. Indy pulled harder, tugging, jerking, until he nearly fell off the side of the train.

Shivering, Indy clung to the windowsill, wondering what to do now. Wait—the window! He levered his free hand against the frame, inching the window up. Finally, he had it open enough to crawl back inside.

Indy collapsed on the compartment floor, taking a few deep breaths. At last, he pulled himself together enough to get to his feet, open the compartment door, and step into the corridor.

Ahead of him was the doorway to the next carriage.

And standing there was Charles Gorham.

"That stupid fool of a Wace," the mine

manager growled at Indy. "I thought you'd get round him." Gorham's hand went into his pocket, and he pulled out a Webley pistol. "Now, you little brat, *I'll* . . ."

Indy didn't wait to hear more. He turned and ran for the far end of the carriage. Throwing the door open, he leapt onto the platform between carriages.

His heart sank. Coming back down the next carriage was Eric Wace. Indy was caught between the two men who wanted to kill him. He looked out between the two cars, and even there he saw no escape. The train was moving slowly, but it was crossing a bridge. He couldn't jump from the train without landing in a river.

He glanced from one advancing enemy to the other. Maybe, just maybe . . .

Wace saw Indy through the window of the door, and began running toward him. Another second and I'm done for, Indy thought. He threw himself off to the right, holding on to the waist-high guardrail. At last, they had passed the bridge. While the train was still moving slowly Indy jumped off.

He landed among the flinty pebbles of the track bed, tumbling to his knees. A second later, he was back on his feet, running as fast as he could. Behind him, he heard shouting. Gorham and Wace had met on the platform between carriages. A shot rang out, and Indy threw himself to the ground. There was a little gully there, which gave him some cover.

Keeping as low as he could, Indy peered back at the train. Another moment or two, and his pursuers would be out of range. He could see the two men in the light from the two carriages, arguing on the platform. Wace had grabbed the gun away from Gorham. Gesturing violently, Gorham pointed toward Indy. Then he pushed Wace off the train.

Indy was up and running again before Wace even hit the track bed. He now had a desperate man with a gun after him. No way was Indy going to try crossing the railroad bridge with a gun at his back. He couldn't even follow the tracks to the next station. Wace was ahead of him there, blocking that path.

I've got no choice, Indy decided. I'll set off cross-country, and hope I reach some kind of safety. He remembered how winded Wace had gotten just running down the hill after the runaway wagon. Maybe Indy would be able to lose the man in the darkness.

The fields that Indy cut across were low-lying and marshy, freshly mown—and absolutely empty of any cover. At least, Wace didn't have good light to aim by. There was only the thinnest crescent of new moon this night. Indy blundered along for miles, hardly able to see where he was going.

Bursting out of one of the hedgerows that bounded a field, Indy found himself tumbling down into a ditch.

A road! he realized, tiredly pulling himself to his feet again. That means somewhere along here there's either a farmhouse—or a town.

He broke into a stumbling trot, blindly following the road. It seemed to be leading toward a large, dark mass ahead. Indy's heart sank. If he was going into the hills, he was heading away from the towns. He looked back toward a small rise, and saw a black figure outlined against the crescent moon. Wace was still on his trail.

No choice. Indy forced his tired feet to plod onward. How he was going to get up this hill, he wasn't sure.

As he came closer the looming mass got a little clearer. It also, strangely, began to look familiar. There was something about the way the sides of the hill didn't just slope up, but rose like steps . . .

Then Indy realized—he'd seen the hill before, while he was chugging past on the train with Cerdic. This was Cadbury Castle, the ancient hill-fort. What was it that Cerdic had told him?

Frankly, Indy was too tired to try to remember. He was just happy that the road here rose in a gentle slope. It led toward some sort of gap at the crest of the hill. There were trees up there. Maybe he could find a hiding place—

Indy froze, listening intently. He wasn't sure. But wasn't that a new sound? There it was again. A faint, muffled *clip-clop*. Yes, it was the sound of a horse's hoofs hitting the ground.

Maybe someone was coming along. Maybe they could offer Indy a ride—or at least get him out of Wace's range.

The odd thing about the sound, though, was that Indy couldn't quite pinpoint where it was coming from. Was it someone heading down from the hill, ahead of him? Or was the lone rider behind Indy, heading toward the hill—just as Wace was doing?

There seemed to be more hoofbeats, as if there were a number of horses on the road. Indy stared a little wildly, straining his eyes. Where were these horses? From the sounds, they seemed to be approaching him. But there was nothing on the road—no one but Wace and his gun.

Giving up his hopes of rescue, Indy started heading up the road again. There were still the trees—and now there was some mist on the road. Or was it? No, this wasn't a fog bank. It seemed to be—Indy wasn't sure *what* it was. There seemed to be individual figures . . . figures riding horses. But he could see the trees behind these phantoms. It was as if they were ghosts.

That triggered the memory of Cerdic's story back on the train. Every seven years, ghosts were supposed to ride down from Cadbury Castle. When was that supposed to happen? Samhain, Celtic New Year's Eve— Halloween. Then Indy realized what today's date was. Tonight was Halloween—this was the night of the ghosts!

Chapter 9

Indy scrambled off the road as the misty figures came closer. A wave of cold suddenly hit him like a wall. It was as if the air suddenly froze to very clear ice. Indy felt himself moving more slowly as a long procession of ghostly riders passed him.

Although he couldn't see details, it seemed as if most of the phantoms were bent over their horses. Were they tired? Had they already ridden for miles? Years? Centuries? Why were they here?

It must have something to do with that

ancient feast Samhain—the night when spirits roam the earth. Frankly, Indy was glad to see the last of the ghostly riders pass him. This was getting altogether too eerie.

But the last rider *didn't* pass. It reined in its horse, turning toward Indy. He stood frozen, staring back. The phantom was still a creature of mist, but Indy felt blue eyes on him. No, they weren't looking at him. They were looking at the ring on Indy's finger— the ancient silver dragon ring he'd found with Cerdic.

The next thing Indy knew, he was walking toward the road. And the misty figure was holding out a hand to him. His own hand, with the ring on it, reached up.

Indy couldn't believe he was doing this. He expected his hand to pass through the ghost's. Instead, he felt a tremendous shock. The freezing chill suddenly left his bones— and he found himself holding a soft, warm hand.

He stared up—not at a misty figure, but at a beautiful young woman. She wore a white undertunic with a blue gown. A hooded woolen mantle covered her shoulders and her chestnut hair. A silver pin glinted on her shoulder, and her bright blue eyes looked hard at him.

Indy stared around in shock. The woods he'd seen on the slopes of Cadbury Castle had disappeared. Now the hill rose in a series of ramparts, topped by a stone-and-timber wall with wooden towers. But there was something wrong in the fortress. Indy could see fire blazing from the middle of the fortified area. Flames rose higher than the towers of the outer defenses.

"What happened to me?" Indy asked the beautiful woman.

She looked baffled, then said something in a musical foreign language with a lot of odd sounds. Realizing he didn't understand, she leaned forward in her saddle until her finger touched Indy's forehead.

"Do you understand me now, Young Jones?" the woman asked.

Indy stared in shock. "H-how did you do that?" he asked.

She smiled. "It seems Morgen's poor powers are no longer known in your time."

"They sure as heck impress me," Indy told

her. "What do you mean, my time? Have I gone back to the past?"

"In a way," Morgen said. "Certainly you are not in 1913." She shook her head. "Come."

Indy scrambled onto Morgen's bay horse, settling himself behind her. She kicked her heels against the bay's sides, urging the horse to catch up with the cavalcade ahead of them.

The other riders weren't ghosts anymore. They were people—mainly women in mantles, some warriors in crested helmets that covered most of their faces. And they all looked tired.

Before Indy was able to ask Morgen about them, she turned to him with a strange look. "There," she said, pointing to the side of the road.

Indy followed her finger, to see a shapeless shadow, a patch of mist beside the path.

"That is the one who pursued you," Morgen told him. "He does not see you now."

"You must see him a lot more clearly than I do," Indy said.

Morgen shrugged. "I have the fey powers—the Second Sight. That is how I noticed you—and know some other things. Tell me, Young Jones, how did that ring you wear come onto your hand?"

Indy stumbled through an explanation of his adventures of the last few days. Some of it Morgen had a hard time understanding.

"I have powers," she said, "but I do not know everything. Huge mines for the blackstone? Great engines that thunder across the land? The sons of Angles and Saxons ruling Britain—even unto the West and North? This is a fascinating—but sad—story you tell me, Young Jones." She sighed. "Though not so surprising, with all the disasters that have fallen on us."

"What's going on?" Indy asked. "Why are you leaving here?"

"The end of our world," Morgen said. Her face held a look of untold sadness. "The Grail lost, the High King dead, and now Camlann, our great fortress, is destroyed by traitors."

Hearing her words, Indy couldn't help but think of the legends his father had told him about, and the things he'd learned on this trip. Camlann—it sounded tantalizingly like Camelot, King Arthur's fortress. A Grail—the Holy Grail? Dad had written a book about that. And a High King—Indy had talked about that with Cerdic Sandyford.

"Who is the High King?" Indy asked.

Morgen reined in her horse in shock. "That *my* name is forgotten—well, the years are long. But surely the name of Artorius has survived?"

"He's still remembered," Indy told her, "but by the name of Arthur. And you haven't been forgotten either, Morgen." He'd just remembered that some stories about King Arthur told of a woman with magic powers—Morgan le Fay! But she was shown as an enemy, not a friend of Camelot. As Morgen had said, the years are long. Maybe the stories changed.

"If Camelot—Camlann—is gone, what will you do?" he asked.

"The few of us who escape will accompany the queen, Gwenhwyfar," Morgen said. Indy nodded. Guinevere was Arthur's queen in the stories. "But first, we must hide

Artorius' treasures. I thought we could use the gold to build new armies and fight again. But from what you tell me, Young Jones, I think our cause is doomed."

The riders came up to a river. Indy looked at the shores. Was this where he leapt from the train? There was no bridge, but there was a ford. The cavalcade stopped as the riders let their horses drink.

From behind them, Indy suddenly heard a shout of victory, and the pounding of many feet. Morgen turned in her saddle, her face grim.

"The enemy did not stay to loot Camlann. They follow us for the treasure—and to kill all of Artorius' people."

The pursuers were mostly dressed in leather armor, with ragged wool breeches. They looked more like robbers than a regular army. Maybe they were. Indy could understand some of their shouts—they were in the same language Morgen used. Other shouts and orders sounded more like German. Was this how English sounded when it first was spoken in this land?

Wheeling her horse around, Morgen made

some complicated gestures in the air. Designs seemed to glow after her fingers, and the air suddenly became very cold. Morgen moved her arm as if she were throwing something—and suddenly the road was filled with monsters.

Some were nearly human creatures, with too many heads, or animal heads, or several parts of animals put together. Indy saw a snake with a bear's head, and a dragon breathing fire.

The armed rabble drew back, frightened by the strange creatures confronting them. Morgen's face was set in strain. "They are only dreams—illusions. And they will not hold these ones long."

Indy hoped they'd last long enough. Behind them, the tired escapees from Camelot were thundering off on their horses.

Morgen was only too right in her prediction. One warrior, braver than the others, swung a huge battle-ax at the dragon. It passed right through, cutting thin air. "Come, brothers!" the warrior yelled. "These are not real!"

He plowed through Morgen's army of illusion, and came straight for the sorceress, his ax held high.

Indy couldn't hold still. He leapt from the horse, placing himself between Morgen and the warrior. Something felt very wrong. As soon as he jumped, the world became wavery, unreal. The ax-toting warrior obviously saw him, though.

Moving faster than Indy would have believed, the man switched his attack from Morgen. He sent the weapon swinging for Indy's chest—and there was no way to duck.

Chapter 10

Indy stood frozen as the ax blade reached him—*but it passed right through him,* as if it were only a ghost weapon! Or was Indy now the ghost?

The warrior sneered, obviously thinking Indy was only another illusion. Indy knew he had to do something before Morgen was chopped down. He grabbed for the handle of the ax. He *had* to be real enough to save Morgen. He *had* to stop this guy.

Maybe it was his wishing, maybe it was his will. But the handle suddenly felt solid enough under his hands. He jerked at the weapon, and it flew from the warrior's grasp. The fighting man fell back, his scarred face now filling with superstitious fear.

Then he turned tail and ran, screaming warnings to his friends. "Back, back! The witch tricks us into her clutches. The vile beasts are real!"

Morgen charged her horse after the terrified warrior, and sent him and his fellow robbers scattering. She then pulled back on the reins, however, grabbing frantically for Indy.

He was glad she did. The whole world seemed to be disappearing in a shimmering mist. As soon as he felt her hand again, though, everything became real.

"Don't leave me again like that, Young Jones. I nearly lost you."

"L-lost me?" Indy's throat felt very dry.

"You would have become lost between the worlds—a ghost, I think you would call it."

Indy stayed very close to Morgen as they crossed the river and caught up with the cavalcade. After riding for miles, the fleeing

Britons had stopped between two rocks. Or rather, Indy realized, one rock that looked as if it had been sliced in two by a gigantic sword.

The stones were a good twenty feet tall, making an excellent landmark. And right in front of the cleft, several British warriors had dug a pit. Now they were unloading boxes and bags of gold and silver—Arthur's treasure—to be hidden in the ground.

Indy craned his neck over Morgen's shoulder, staring in fascination. She had to repeat herself twice to get his attention.

"Young Jones," she said, "this far only may you travel with us. We must leave you here, but I think you will find friends nearby."

Indy prepared to dismount. He felt sad to say good-bye to Morgen, and a little disappointed, too. If only he'd been his father—what questions he'd have been able to ask!

Morgen smiled, as if reading his mind. "Your father will find what your father will find," she said cryptically. "And you'll do well enough, Young Jones. Guard that ring you wear." She touched the dragon ring on

Indy's finger. For a second, it grew warm. "And remember—it once belonged to Artorius the King."

Indy gawked at the silver ring. "Then how did it wind up inside the rock at Arthur's Fountain?"

Morgen smiled, and drew a silver chain from around her neck, underneath her mantle. Hanging from the end of the chain was a shining ring, the twin to the one Indy wore. Indy felt the short hairs rise on the back of his neck. No, not a twin. It was the *same* ring as the one he wore.

"I know the place," Morgen said. "The great crag with the twisted sapling on the top. Rest assured, it will be hidden there."

Standing on the ground, still holding Morgen's hand, Indy stared up at the beautiful woman. "Farewell, Young Jones," she said. "I must join the other riders."

Morgen let go of his hand, and she and all the others became figures of mist again. They rode off, all slowly vanishing, until only one was left—a vague shape that suddenly turned back and waved good-bye.

Indy felt sad. Although Morgan le Fay might be a villainess in the stories, he now knew that Morgen definitely fought on the side of good.

He turned back to the rocks where the treasure was hidden—and stared in surprise. In a way, almost fifteen hundred years had passed since he'd last seen this spot. The cleft rock appeared feet shorter, and trees had seemingly sprung up from nowhere. The best part, though, was that Indy could see lights in the distance. He ran toward them, and found an old timbered manor house. Here he could get help!

Indy ran to the front door and rapped the brass knocker. "Did you get what you needed, Doctor?" a voice asked as the door opened. "Indy, what are you doing here?"

Indiana Jones looked just as dumbfounded. Standing in the doorway was Cerdic Sandyford.

The Sandyford estate was so full of confusion and worry that no one else even noticed that Indy was there. "We found a telegram from Charles Gorham waiting for us when we arrived," Cerdic said to Indy. "He's taken over several loans Father took out to replace equipment for the mine. With the colliery shut down, there's no way we can repay them. Gorham's coming to foreclose."

Cerdic's hands were tightly clenched into fists as he passed on this information. "He's going to make sure we're put out of business."

"Maybe not as sure as he thinks," Indy said, drawing his friend outside. "Do you know where we could find a couple of shovels at this time of night?"

Back at the cleft rock, they dug down until the hole they'd made was as deep as they were tall. As he kept digging a horrible thought struck Indiana Jones. What if the treasure they were looking for had been dug up already? After all, a thousand years and almost half as much again had passed. Maybe Morgen and her friends had come back ages ago, dug up the gold, and outfitted a new army to carry on the fight.

That was the exact moment when Cerdic's shovel clunked against something. Down on their knees, they uncovered the obstruction. It was a thick silver plaque.

Cerdic gasped. "Indy, do you know what this means?" he asked joyfully.

"I said I'd catch up to you." A voice from above them cut short the celebration.

Eric Wace stood at the top of their pit, Gorham's gun in his hand. A weird, unpleasant smile spread across his face.

"And look at all the work you've saved me—digging your own grave."

Chapter 11

Eric Wace stared down at Indy and Cerdic triumphantly. Then, for the first time, he seemed to realize why they were down in the pit they'd created.

"What have you got there?" Wace demanded.

"Nothing much," Indy told him. "Just treasure."

"Treasure?" Wace's pale eyes gleamed with greed.

"Sure, you know. Treasure. Gold. Silver. Maybe some jewels. Pretty much the usual thing." Indy continued to dig with his hands.

Something gave under his fingers. He found a leather pouch, rotted away. It was filled with gold coins. "Want some?" Indy asked, drawing it out of the ground.

"Give it here." Wace gestured with his gun.

"With pleasure." Indy flung the bag and coins into Wace's face.

The two boys moved together while the gunman was temporarily blinded. They jumped to their feet, leapt for the top of the pit they'd dug—and grabbed Eric Wace's ankles.

Wace didn't even have time to pull the trigger before they dragged him down into the hole. It was a confusing fight. All of them rolled around in the moist earth, but the two boys continued to work as a team. Indy went for Wace's gun hand, fighting to get the weapon free. Cerdic concentrated on hitting any part of Wace that showed.

Roaring and sputtering, Wace finally broke free of Indy's hold. "Now I'll—"

He never got any farther with his snarled threat. Cerdic beaned him with the heavy silver plaque, and Wace went down like a felled tree.

Indy pulled the unconscious man's belt free. "Let's tie him up," he suggested. "Then we can finish getting this treasure out."

They came back to the manor house carrying as much as they could, and leading a bound Eric Wace. Even as they came in the front door they could hear the blustering voice of Charles Gorham.

"No, ma'am, the house *won't* be enough. I want it all. The savings, the house, the land. I trust this will teach you not to get on the wrong side of Charles Gorham."

Indy strode into the parlor where Gorham was threatening Mrs. Sandyford. "The problem with you, Gorham, is that you haven't got a *right* side," Indy said.

"You!" Gorham goggled at Indy. "What are you doing here?"

"Well, first, I thought I'd take care of Mr. Sandyford's debts." Indy plunked down an armload of gold coins. "And second, I thought you should know that the guy you sent to take care of me didn't do his job."

Eric Wace was pushed through the doorway, flanked by a husky pair of farm boys.

Gorham's fat, flabby face flushed red as he yelled at his agent. "You stupid fool! Can't even handle a mere boy! What do I pay you for . . ."

His voice died out as he realized what he'd said.

"That's exactly the question," Cerdic said, coming into the room with another armload of treasure. "What *were* you paying Eric Wace for? Closing down our mine? Nearly killing my father? Trying to kill my friend?"

Wace, dirty and disheveled, shook some mud out of his blond hair. He could see which way things were going. "It's all *his* fault," the young man said, staring at Gorham. "Everything I did, I did at his orders."

"You stupid fool!" Gorham yelled. "I should have let you rot when they threw you out of the army. But no, I had to go and hire you . . ."

The two were still at their argument when the county constables arrived nearly half an hour later. By the time they were carried off to the jail, each was falling all over himself to blame the other.

Indy was tired—this had been a very long

night. But he and Cerdic still had work to do. They went back out to the pit. Working by lamplight, and with the help of the farm boys, they kept digging until they'd gotten up everything that had been buried there.

By the next day, the gold and silver had been all sorted out on the dining-room table. Word of the discovery had gotten out. The newspapermen—and professors from nearby universities—began arriving.

"Definitely late Roman," one of the great names of British archeology said, examining the plaque with a magnifying glass. "And many of the coins seem to be Roman-British. This is quite a Dark Age hoard you boys have uncovered."

He shook his head, taking in all the gold and silver on the table. "Where did you get the idea to go digging in front of that cleft rock?"

"That's a long story," Indy said quickly. And one this guy wouldn't believe, he thought. How could I tell him a ghost showed me where to dig?

"We think it may be King Arthur's treasury," Indy finally went on. "Suppose there really was a fortress on the top of Cadbury Castle. The people may have had to leave, and could have hidden the treasure here—"

"King Arthur!" the professor burst out, as if Indy had started talking about fairy tales.

"I suppose I shouldn't be surprised," the man said more gently. "Mention the Dark Ages in Britain, and most people bring up the name of King Arthur." He shook his head. "Let me give you a few words of advice, though, before you start talking to the newspapers. Do you have anything written that connects this treasure to Arthur? Was there anything buried here to suggest it?"

"You said yourself that this is a Roman-British treasure," Indy began.

"And dozens, maybe *hundreds* of treasures like this have been dug up over the years," the professor said. "Are you suggesting Arthur buried them all? Remember, this was a time of war and raiding. Many people buried their gold and silver to hide it from the invaders. And a lot of it was never recovered."

The archeologist gave Indy a sharp glance.

"Or did you find something with Arthur's name on it? That would be a real discovery. It doesn't have to be a metal plate carved with 'Here lies Arthur's treasure.' I'd be satisfied just to find a coin with his name on it. We don't even have that, you know. All we know about Arthur are the spoken stories that were passed down. If there's a real piece of proof you can produce . . ."

Indy shook his head. Cerdic and his family would have to be happy with the treasure and the story they could pass down. Indy had told Cerdic everything, Morgen and all. Cerdic at least believed. He had the treasure as proof. But it was just too unbelievable to try convincing the scientists and newsmen.

As evening came on, Indy got ready to head for the train station. His brief vacation was ending—he'd be due back at Charenton in the morning. Indy would be traveling alone, though. Cerdic had already explained how he had to stay at home. Although the treasure took care of the Sandyfords' financial problems, there was still much to be done. Mr. Sandyford was out of his coma, but had to be cared for until he regained his health. At least, there was more optimism about that. "Besides, old bean," Cerdic had said, "I'm the man of the family for the time being. It's up to me to take care of the family business."

He had the good grace to look a little embarrassed. "Or at least, help Mother look after the business. It looks like we have the money to reopen the mine. I've wired the good news to Trewen already."

"I'm glad," Indy told him.

"But what about you?" Cerdic said. "You won't accept any reward for helping us, or a fair share of the treasure . . ."

"Since you don't want me to leave empty-handed, I'll tell you what," Indy suggested. "Suppose I take this"—he picked up a gold Roman *denarius* coin—"as a souvenir. But then I have to give something to you."

Tugging at his finger, Indy loosened the silver dragon ring.

"Oh no," Cerdic insisted. "I couldn't take that. After all, I gave it to you when you saved Father's life."

"But I think it belongs here," Indy said.

"Somewhere in my wanderings last night, an odd memory popped into my head. I remembered my father reading from this old book from France—Brittany. It was stories of King Arthur, but stories I'd never heard before. Dad had a hard time making some of it out. There was one line in particular that threw him. It mentioned King Arthur, then Prince Cerdic."

Cerdic frowned in puzzlement. "What are you saying?" he asked.

Indy shrugged. "You told me Cerdic is an old British name. Maybe your family is closer to Arthur than you think."

His friend stared at the silver dragon in awe. "Arthur's ring," Cerdic breathed. "What a strange route it took to get here."

A little chill ran down Indy's spine. "Maybe that's the way it was meant to be," he said. "The ring led us to the treasure. It's almost as if it had been planned out, to save you when you needed it the most."

If his theory about Cerdic being descended from Arthur was right, it was only fair that the king's ring—and gold—should now save Arthur's distant kinsman.

"Planned?" Cerdic said, bemused, as Indy dropped the ring into his hand. "Planned by whom?"

As the ring left Indy's fingers he seemed to hear a ghostly tinkle of laughter. He knew that voice.

It was the laughter of Morgan le Fay.

HISTORICAL NOTE

King Arthur is one of Britain's greatest heroes—in spite of the fact that no one knows if he really existed. The problem is that Arthur lived in the early Dark Ages. That was when history and learning—even reading and writing—disappeared.

Sixteen hundred years ago, Britain was a part of the Roman Empire, a very rich and civilized country. By the year 410, however, Roman troops had been pulled out of Britain to fight other wars. The Britons would have to face invaders—Germanic tribes known as Angles, Saxons, and Jutes—alone.

For forty years, the barbarians ravaged the land. They burned cities and enslaved the people. It was a terrifying, confused time, with no records left. Finally, however, the Britons rallied. Their stories tell of defeating the invaders in twelve great battles. And their *Dux Bellorum,* Latin for "Leader of Wars," was a man called Artorius—Arthur, in English.

Was he real? Or did later storytellers lump together several British leaders into one character? Archeologists are now sure that for forty years, the Angles and Saxons did not expand their lands. In fact, they could not. Partly that was because of a strong wall of hill-forts—like Cadbury Castle.

Local legends say this is the site of Camelot, King Arthur's capital. An archeologist did dig there in 1913, and found some ancient remains. A major dig in the 1960s found traces of the fortress with the stone-and-timber walls described in this book. The discoveries caused a great stir. But the archeologists found no proof to link the site to Arthur.

The peace in Britain did not last forever. By the year 500, the march of Anglo-Saxon victories started again. Today the largest country in Great Britain is Angle-land—England.

The tales of Arthur did not go away, however. They were kept alive wherever the ancient Britons survived—Scotland, Wales, Cornwall, and Brittany (Little Britain) in France. There are many places called Arthur's Well and Arthur's Throne, named after the great hero.

The French-speaking Normans conquered England in 1066. They learned of the Arthur stories—and began retelling them. All through the later Middle Ages, the stories grew and characters changed. Morgen, for instance, who was a friendly magical helper to Arthur, became in later stories Morgan le Fay, an evil witch. Whole new characters, like Sir Lancelot, were added. King Arthur and his Round Table became knights in shining armor.

The stories are still told today, in books and movies. Sometimes they show Arthur in the heavy plate armor of the 1300s, eight hundred years after he would have died. Sometimes they show him as a Roman soldier, or a British chief, fighting barbarians.

However he appears, Arthur remains one of the most inspiring heroes of literature. Although his people lost their war, and he himself is a legend, his memory lives on, while leaders more real—and more successful—have been forgotten.

TO FIND OUT MORE, CHECK OUT . . .

Did Arthur really exist, or was he just a legend? The following three books try to answer this question.

King Arthur in Fact and Legend by Geoffrey Ashe. Published by Thomas Nelson, 1971. Both the fictional and historical Arthur are explored. Includes interesting archaeological facts about excavations at South Cadbury, the possible site of the original Camelot. Photographs, drawings.

Quest for a King—Searching for the Real King Arthur by Catherine M. Andronik. Published by Atheneum, 1989. The author retells the fictional stories of Arthur, and offers different people's theories to explain how the legends grew out of real events in history. Very readable. Photographs, drawings, map.

The Search for King Arthur by Christopher Hibbert. Published by American Heritage Publishing Co., 1969. Covers various Arthurian legends and stories and how they have changed over the years. Extensively illustrated with photographs, drawings, maps, many in color.

The Landscape of King Arthur by Geoffrey Ashe. Photographs by Simon McBride. Published by Henry Holt and Company, 1988. *In Ghostly Riders,* Indy saw and heard about many places associated with Arthur and his world—including Cadbury Castle, Camlann, Somerset, and more. In this lavishly illustrated book, you can see where Indy's travels took him. Beautiful photographs, many in color.

Wales (Enchantment of the World series) by Dorothy B. Sutherland. Published by Children's Press, 1987. Indy got a brief introduction to Wales when he visited the Sandyford home and colliery. This book will tell you a great deal more about this fascinating country—its history, geography, industries, and language. Gives you a good sense of the land and its people. Photographs, drawings, maps, many in color.

SHARE THE ADVENTURE!

THE LUCASFILM FAN CLUB

Follow the adventures of Young Indiana Jones through the pages of The Official Lucasfilm Fan Club Magazine. Each issue has exclusive features, behind-the-scene articles and interviews on the people who make the *Indiana Jones* films as well as *Star Wars!* Plus there are special articles on the Disney theme-park spectaculars, Lucasfilm Games as well as Industrial Light & Magic — the special effects wizards! You can also purchase genuine collectors items through the club's official catalog such as theater one-sheets, toys, clothing, as well as products made exclusively for members only!

YOUR MEMBERSHIP INCLUDES:
A fantastic 10th anniversary *Empire Strikes Back* Membership Kit including:
- Exclusive *ESB* One-Sheet (originally created for *ESB,* but never produced!)
- Embroidered Fan Club Jacket Patch!
- Two *ESB* 8x10 full color photos!
- *Star Wars* Lives bumper sticker!
- Welcome letter from George Lucas!
- Full-color Membership Card!

PLUS:
- One-year subscription to the quarterly full-color Lucasfilm Magazine!
- Cast and crew fan mail forwarding!
- Classified section (for sale, wanted & pen pals section!)
- Science Fiction convention listing!
- And more!

JOIN FOR ONLY $9.95